Archibald MacNeill

Notes on the Authenticity of Ossian's Poems

Archibald MacNeill

Notes on the Authenticity of Ossian's Poems

ISBN/EAN: 9783337397913

Printed in Europe, USA, Canada, Australia, Japan

Cover: Foto ©Andreas Hilbeck / pixelio.de

More available books at **www.hansebooks.com**

NOTES

HE AUTHENTICITY

OF

OSSIAN'S POEMS

BY

A MEMBER OF THE SOCIETY OF ANTIQUARIES

OF SCOTLAND

" I've stood upon Achilles' tomb
And heard Troy doubted; time will doubt of Rome."
—Byron.

PRINTED FOR THE AUTHOR

1868

NOTES

AUTHENTICITY OF OSSIAN'S POEMS.

THE publication of the Dean of Lismore's book has thrown additional light on the Ossianic controversy, and added fresh proofs of the authenticity of these poems. This manuscript, which is in the form of a quarto volume of some 311 pages, was written in the Gaelic language by the Dean of Lismore and his brother, betwixt 1512 and 1529, and contains upwards of 11,000 lines of Gaelic poetry, composed at different periods, 2500 of which are Ossianic. The latter are contained in 28 poems, 9 of which are directly attributed to Ossian, the others to different bards of the Feine. It forms one of the 65 Gaelic MSS. now collected in the Library of the Faculty of Advocates at Edinburgh, through the instrumentality of Mr Skene.

The contents of this volume, though alluded to in Report of the Highland Society's Committee, were unknown to the public, and would have probably remained so, had it not been for the perseverance and industry of the Rev. Dr Maclachlan in deciphering, transcribing, and translating it. He has thus not only made accessible to the public many additional pieces of that class of poetry of which James Macpherson was the most successful collector, but afforded additional proof of the accuracy with which the Ossianic poems have been orally transmitted for generations; for many of the pieces collected by the Dean of Lismore from recitation in 1512, were also so collected by Mr Duncan Kennedy, with very little variation, nearly three centuries afterwards, as appears from the MS. collection made by that gentleman betwixt the years 1774 and 1783, which was purchased by the Highland Society of Scotland, and is now in the Advocates' Library at Edinburgh.

Before entering into further detail as to the contents of the Dean of Lismore's volume, and their bearing on the Ossianic controversy, it may be necessary to trace shortly the circumstances under which James Macpherson was induced to undertake the collection of the remains of Gaelic poetry, and the manner in which it was accomplished.

James Macpherson was born at Ruthven, in the county of Inverness, in the year 1738. He was descended from one of the oldest families in the north of Scotland, being nearly related to the chief of the clan Macpherson. He received the rudiments of his education at Inverness Grammar School; from thence he was removed to King's College, Aberdeen, and eventually to Edinburgh University, where he completed his studies.[*]

* See Highland Soc. Report (cited in the notes that follow as H. S. R.) p. 27.

In 1759, while tutor to Mr Graham of Balgowan (afterwards Lord Lynedoch), he met at Moffat with Mr John Home (the author of 'Douglas'), who had previously been told by Professor Adam Ferguson, a native of Athole, and acquainted with Gaelic, that there existed in the Highlands some remains of ancient Gaelic poetry. Mr Home mentioned the circumstance to James Macpherson, and was told by him that he had some pieces of ancient Gaelic poetry in his possession. After some difficulty, Mr Home obtained translations of two of these from Macpherson, took them to Edinburgh, and showed them to Drs Blair, Ferguson, and Robertson, by whom they were much admired. Macpherson was requested to translate all he had, being fifteen in number; and the translations furnished by him were published by Dr Blair, with a preface, in June 1760, in a little volume, under the title of 'Fragments of Ancient Poetry, collected in the Highlands of Scotland.' Soon after this publication, a subscription was set on foot to defray the expense of collecting the remains of ancient Gaelic poetry, and a dinner-party was got up, to which Macpherson was invited, with the view of inducing him to undertake a journey to the Highlands for that purpose.* At this dinner-party, among others, there were present Drs Blair, Robertson, and Ferguson, Mr John Home, Mr Robert Chalmers, and Patrick, Lord Elibank. Macpherson agreed to undertake the collection, but not without considerable reluctance, as he feared that the search might prove unsuccessful to an extent that might disappoint his friends.

* See Blair's Letter, H. S. R., p. 56.

He soon afterwards set out on his journey, and was accompanied during a great portion of it by two countrymen of his own, Mr Lachlan Macpherson of Strathmashie, a native of Badenoch, and Ewan Macpherson, formerly a schoolmaster in Badenoch, both of whom were much better Gaelic scholars than himself. He was afterwards joined and assisted by another Gaelic scholar, Captain Alexander Morison.

In this tour a number of MSS. were collected, and much Gaelic poetry was taken down from recitation, as we shall presently show.

On his return, Macpherson proceeded to Badenoch, which was his own native place, as well as that of Lachlan Macpherson, and there remained till January 1761,* engaged, with the assistance of Lachlan Macpherson and the Rev. Mr Gallie, then a missionary in Badenoch, in preparing the materials for the next publication of the remains of Ossianic poetry. He then proceeded to Edinburgh, from whence he writes to the Rev. James M'Lagan a letter dated 16th January 1761.†

His task, so far as the arrangements of the Gaelic originals was concerned, had, it appears, been then accomplished ; and, during his stay in Edinburgh, he seems to have been engaged in translating and in preparing the English version for the press.‡ So soon as this was completed he went to London, and, early in 1762, he there published a quarto volume, containing the epic of 'Fingal' in six books, and fifteen minor poems—viz., 'Comala,' 'The War of Caros,' 'The War of Innis-Thona,' 'The Battle of Lora,' 'Conlath and Cuthona,' 'Carthon,' 'The Death of Cuthullen,' 'Darthula,' 'Carricthura,' 'The Songs of Selma,' 'Calthon and Commal,' 'Lathmon,' 'Oithona,' 'Croma,' and 'Berathon.' In the following year he published another quarto, containing another epic in eight books, called 'Temora,' and five minor poems. This volume contained also what was called a specimen of the original of 'Temora,' being a Gaelic version of the seventh book of that poem, and the only Gaelic bearing to be the original of any of the poems which appeared. The minor poems were, 'Cuthlin of Clutha,' 'Sulmala of Lummon,' 'Cath-Loda,' 'Oina-Morul,' 'Colna-Dona.'

The favourable reception given to these works is well known. It is sufficient here to observe that they were, in the first year after their publication, translated into almost all the languages of Europe.

Macpherson was soon assailed by scepticism as to the Gaelic origin of the poetry he professed to have translated; and though he declined to appeal to those who had aided him in the collection and translation of the poems, yet he furnished Dr Blair* with their names, and consented to his applying to them. He also placed the original MSS. in the hands of Mr Becket, the London bookseller, and notified to the public by advertisement that he had done so.

In 1764 Macpherson accompanied Governor Johnstone to Pensacola, and after holding the official appointment of President of Council at West Florida, he returned to England in 1766.

---

* See Blair's Letter, App. H. S. R., p. 60.

In 1769 he was, on the resignation of Sir John Macpherson, appointed agent to the Nawab of Arcot, in which situation he amassed a large fortune. Through Sir John's interest he was returned to Parliament for the burgh of Camelford, which he continued to represent for some years. Towards the close of his life he removed to Belleville, a seat he had bought in his native county, where he died in 1796, and was, in accordance with his own request, buried in Westminster Abbey.

By his settlement he left John Mackenzie, Esq., of the Temple, one of his executors, and bequeathed L.1000 * for the purpose of defraying the expense of preparing for the press and publishing in the original Gaelic the Ossianic poems he had collected, a portion of which he had previously handed to Mr Mackenzie. The manuscripts written in Gaelic which came into the possession of Mr Mackenzie were not ancient manuscripts ; they were in the handwriting of Macpherson himself, or of others whom he had employed to take down the poetry from recitation, or to copy it from the MSS. with which he had been furnished during his tour. Of the old manuscripts collected by him none were found in his repositories, with the exception of one small duodecimo manuscript belonging to Clanronald, written by one of the M'Vurichs, and which was returned.

That Macpherson obtained many Gaelic manuscripts during his search in the Highlands in 1760 there can be no doubt. This appears distinctly from the evidence of those who assisted in their collection and translation,

* See Diss. by Sir John Sinclair, prefixed to Highland Society's Edition of Ossian, p. 92.

and was fully elicited by Dr Blair and by a Committee of the Highland Society appointed for the purpose. In 1763 Dr Blair addressed letters to many of those gentlemen requesting specific information on the subject, and also directing that they should each provide themselves with a copy of Macpherson's translations, and having summoned to their presence such parties in their neighbourhood as could recite the poems of Ossian, they should compare these recitations carefully with the translation.

Mr Lachlan Macpherson, writing to Dr Blair from Strathmashie on the 22d October 1763, says : *

"In the year 1760 I had the pleasure of accompanying my friend Mr Macpherson during some part of his journey in search of the poems of Ossian through the Highlands. I assisted him in collecting them, *and took down from oral tradition and transcribed from old manuscripts by far the greatest part of those pieces he has published. I have carefully compared the translation with the copies of the originals in my hands, and find it amazingly literal.* Some of the hereditary bards retained by the chiefs committed very early to writing some of the works of Ossian. *One manuscript in particular was written as far back as the year 1410, which I saw in Mr Macpherson's possession.*"

Mr Angus McNeill, minister of Howmore, in South Uist, in a letter to Dr Blair, dated 22d December 1763, says : †

" Neil McMurrich, a native of this country, who with his predecessors for nineteen generations back have been

* H. S. R., p. 8.   † Id., App., p. 18.

the bards and historians of the family of Clanranald, repeated before me the whole of the poem of 'Darthula or Clan-usneach,' with few variations from the translation, which he deponed he saw and read, together with many more, in a manuscript which underwent the same fate with the manuscript already made mention of. Declared also that he is of opinion the last poem in the collection, 'Berrathon,' is contained in *a manuscript which I myself saw him deliver, with three or four more, to Mr Macpherson when he was in this country,* and for which Mr Macpherson gave him a missive obliging himself to restore them."

Captain A. Morison, in answer to the queries of the Highland Society Committee, writing from Greenock, 7th February 1801, says : *

"That Mr James Macpherson, on his tour through the Highlands and Isles, was a night in his house in Skinnader, Sky. He was then collecting the ancient poems, but when in his house had only a few of them ; that he gave him some, which he afterwards translated and published, together with other Fingalian or old heroic poems not published in his translations, one of them 'Dargo.'

"That he afterwards in London had access to Mr Macpherson's papers,—*saw many MSS. in the old Gaelic character with Mr Macpherson, containing some of the poems translated, which MSS. they found difficult to read.* That he heard of such being in the country. How old the MSS. were cannot say, but from the character and spelling seemed very ancient."

* H. S. R., App., p. 176.

Ewan Macpherson, late schoolmaster at Badenoch, declares before Mr Norman Macdonald, J.P. at Knock, Sleat, Sky, on 11th September 1800,*

"That having come to this country from the opposite coast of Knoydart to pay a visit to the Rev. Dr John Macpherson, then minister of the parish of Sleat, he happened to meet his old acquaintance Mr James Macpherson, who was then employed in collecting the poems of Ossian; and being well acquainted with the Gaelic orthography and character, was urged by James Macpherson to accompany him to the Long Island, which he eventually did.

"That on that occasion they were one or two nights at the house of the elder Clanranald at Ormiglade, and about a week at the house of the younger at Benbicula, and at Mr McNeill's, minister in South Uist, where he became acquainted with MacMhurich, the representative of the celebrated bards of that name, but was not himself a man of any note. From this man the declarant got for Mr James Macpherson *a book* of the size of a Testament, and of the nature of a Common-Place Book, which contained some accounts of the families of the Macdonalds and the exploits of the great Montrose, *together with some of the poems of Ossian.* And Mr Macpherson obtained at the same time an order from Clanranald, sen., on Lieut. Donald Macdonald of Edinburgh, for *a Gaelic folio manuscript* belonging to the family, which was called the 'Leabhar Derg,' and contained, as he heard Clanranald say, some of the poems of Ossian."

* See H. S. R., App., p. 94.

These MSS. the late Mr Macdonald of Clanranald was very anxious to recover from Mr Macpherson, and after an ineffectual correspondence, actually gave directions to Mr William Macdonald, formerly secretary and then treasurer to the Highland Society, to bring an action for their recovery : this, on the understanding that they would be returned by Mr Macpherson, was not followed out.*

The *Rev. Andrew Gallie*, in a letter to Charles Macintosh, Esq., W.S., of date 12th March 1799, says : †

"The translator of Ossian's poems was for some years before he entered on that work my intimate acquaintance and friend. When he returned from his tour through the Western Highlands and Islands, he came to my house in Brae, Badenoch. I inquired the success of his journey, and he produced *several volumes* small octavo, or rather large duodecimo, *in the Gaelic language and characters*, being the poems of Ossian and other ancient bards.

"I remember perfectly that many of those volumes were at the close said to have been collected by Paul MacMhurich, Bard, Clanraonuil, and about the beginning of the fourteenth century. Mr Macpherson and I were of opinion that, though the Bard collected them, yet they must have been writ by an ecclesiastic, for the characters and spelling were most beautiful and correct. Every poem had its first letter of its first word most elegantly flourished and gilded—some red, some yellow, some blue, and some green. The material writ on seemed to be a limber yet coarse and dark vellum.

* See H. S. R., p. 81.   † Id., p. 31.

The volumes were bound in strong parchment. Mr Macpherson had them from Clanronald.

"At that time I could read the Gaelic characters, though with difficulty, and did often amuse myself with reading here and there in those poems while Mr Macpherson was employed on his translation. At times we differed as to the meaning of certain words in the original.

"With much labour I have recovered some scattered parts of the translation made at my fireside—I should rather say of the original translated there, and I communicate to you a few stanzas taken from the manuscript : *

> "'Bha fer re fer, is cruaigh re cruaigh,
> Sgiatha fuaimneach, daoine air lar,
> Mar uird nan ceud air mac nan Eill,
> Dh'eirigh agus theirin gach lann.
> Ghluais Gall mar chrom osaig on aird,
> Gun ghlan e saoighin as.
> Bha Suaran mar chaoir fasàich thall
> Am fraoch fuaimar Gorm-mheall bras.
> Ach cia mur chuiram sios le fonn,
> Bàs trom na n sleagh bha ann?
> Bu scrathoil stri bha san bhlár
> Bu lassach ard mo lann.
> Bu scrathoil Osgar mo mhac fein,
> Thar càch bu treubhach maith!

---

* The Gaelic here is not very correctly written, but the present writer has given it without alteration, as printed in the Highland Society's Report.

Bha sòlas balbh am bhroilleach shuas,
Bhi ghruaigh mar chaoirt san chath.'

"The literal translation of the above passage is as follows :—

"' Man was opposed to man, and steel to steel—
Shields sounding, men falling;
Like hammers of hundreds on the son of the embers
Swords rose and fell.
Gaul went on like a blast descending from the height,
As he destroyed heroes.
Swaran was like a flame of the desert
That consumes the sounding heath of Gormal;
But how shall I relate in song
The heavy death of spears that was there?
Terrible was the strife of battle.
High flamed my sword.
Terrible was Oscar my son,
Whose deeds of valour exceeded all.
Silent joy arose in my breast
As his countenance glowed in the battle.'

"I have not 'Fingal' by me, nor easy access to it, therefore cannot say how these stanzas run in English, but they are sent you as taken out of the manuscript by a friend, who was at the time with Mr Macpherson and me—a gentleman well known for an uncommon acquaintance with the Gaelic, and a happy facility in writing it in the Roman characters. That word marked† was one of those about which different opinions were held, but at last we agreed that it was properly spelled, and did express the fire and rage in Oscar's countenance, while his mind sedate and tranquil regulated his heroism."

Dr Adam Ferguson, Professor of Moral Philosophy in the University of Edinburgh, in answer to the queries of the Highland Society's Committee, says : *

" The fragments I afterwards saw in Mr Macpherson's hands by no means appeared of recent writing. The paper was stained with smoke and daubed with Scots snuff."

The *Rev. Dr Hugh Blair*, Professor of Rhetoric in the University of Edinburgh, says in regard to Mr Macpherson : †

" Accordingly, he soon after set out on his mission through the Highlands, and during the time he was employed in it he wrote to me and others of his friends informing us what success he met with in collecting from many different and remote parts all the remains he could find of ancient Gaelic poetry, either in writing or by oral tradition. When he returned to Edinburgh in winter, laden with his poetical treasures, he took lodgings in a house immediately below where I then lived, at the head of Blackfriars' Wynd, and busied himself *in translating from the Gaelic into English*. I saw him very frequently. He gave me accounts from time to time how he proceeded, and used frequently at dinner to read or repeat to me parts *of what he had that day translated*. Being myself entirely ignorant of the Gaelic language, I never examined or looked into his papers."

* H. S. R., App., p. 63.   † Id., p. 59.

Macpherson himself, writing from Ruthven on 27th October 1760, to the Rev. James M'Lagan, then minister of Amalrie, says : *

" You perhaps have heard that I am employed to make a collection of the ancient poetry in the Gaelic. I have already traversed most of the isles and gathered all worth notice in that quarter.   I intend a journey to Mull and the coast of Argyll to enlarge my collection.

" By letters from Edinburgh, as well as gentlemen of your acquaintance, I am informed that you have a good collection of poems of the kind I want.   It would be therefore very obliging you should transmit me them as soon as convenient, that my book might be rendered more complete and more for the honour of our old poetry.

" Traditions are uncertain : poetry delivered down from memory must lose considerably, and it is a matter of surprise to me how we have now any of the beauties of our ancient Gaelic poetry remaining.

" Your collection, I am informed, is pure, as you have taken pains to restore the style.   I shall not make any apology for this trouble, as it will be for the honour of our ancestors how many of their pieces of genius will be brought to light. *I have met with a number of old manuscripts in my travels: the poetical part of them I have endeavoured to secure.*

" If any of that kind falls within your hearing, I beg it of you to have them in sight.

" Inform me if you can of the tradition of the poems."

* H. S. R., App., p. 153.

Again, writing to Mr M‘Lagan from Edinburgh, 14th January 1761, Macpherson says :*

" I was favoured with your letter enclosing the Gaelic poems, for which I hold myself extremely obliged to you. *Duan a Ghairbh* is less poetical and more obscure than *Tiontach mor na Feine*. The last is far from being a bad poem were it complete, and is particularly valuable for the ancient manners it contains. I shall reckon myself much obliged to you for any other pieces you can send me. It is true I have the most of them from other hands, but the misfortune is that I find none expert in the Irish orthography, so that an obscure poem is rendered doubly so by their uncouth way of spelling.

" I have been lucky enough to lay my hands *on a pretty complete poem, and truly epic, concerning Fingal.* The antiquity of it is easily ascertained, and it is not only superior to anything in that language, but reckoned not inferior to the more polite performances of other nations in that way. I have some thoughts of publishing the original if it will not clog the work too much."

Writing again to Mr M‘Lagan from Edinburgh, on 8th February 1761, he says : †

" I am favoured with your last letter, *enclosing four poems,* for which I am much obliged to you. I beg you send me what more you can conveniently."

From this evidence it is plain that Macpherson was not only diligent in his search, but that he also recovered in his tour and from friends many Gaelic manuscripts containing Ossianic poetry, and some at

* H. S. R., App., p. 154.　　　　† Id., p. 156.

least of an old date; and that up to 1761 there is no
appearance of his having contemplated, and no ground
for supposing that he contemplated, any fraud on the
public. The evidence is all opposed to such a supposition.

But these manuscripts contained only a portion of
the old Gaelic poetry collected by Macpherson. A
great part was acquired from oral recitation. This
appears from the evidence of many who were applied
to by Dr Blair soon after the publication, and some of
whom had accompanied Macpherson on his tour; and
also from the subsequent investigation by the Committee of the Highland Society. The time at which Macpherson made his collection was fortunate, for the reciters of these poems were then passing away; and at
the present day there are few, if any, to be found who
can recite the old heroic poetry, which has given place
to more modern compositions. Even forty years after
Macpherson's tour, when the Committee of the Highland Society commenced their investigation, the reciters
were much reduced in numbers, although even then
enough were found to verify the authenticity of a large
portion of what is comprehended in Macpherson's translations.

Mr Lachlan Macpherson of Strathmashie, already
quoted, writing to Dr Blair in 1763, says,* "*I took
down from oral tradition,* and transcribed from old
manuscripts, by far the greatest part of those pieces he
has published."

Ewan Macpherson, already mentioned, who accompanied Mr Macpherson to Uist, says, that† "On that

* H. S. R., App., p. 8.   † Id., p. 94.

occasion *he was with Mr Macpherson for three or four weeks, in course of which the declarant took down poems of Ossian from the recitations of several individuals, at different places, which he gave to Mr Macpherson, who was seldom present when they were taken down.* That they were generally persons advanced in life."

Captain Alexander Morison, who also assisted Mr Macpherson in collecting and transcribing, says,[*]

"That he does not now remember all the persons who recited or sent them, because he could have no doubt regarding the poems he was accustomed to hear from his infancy. Is certain that Mr Macpherson got some of them from the MacMhurichs in Uist, and some from Mull, and likely from the Fletchers of Glenforsa, famous for a long time for the recitation and history of such poems."

Dr John Macpherson, minister of Sleat, of date 27th November 1763, writing to Dr Blair, says :[†]

"I have, in obedience to your request, made inquiry for all persons around me who were able to rehearse from memory any parts of the poems published by Mr Macpherson, and have made them to rehearse in my hearing the several fragments or detached pieces of these poems which they were able to repeat. This done, I compared with great care the pieces rehearsed by them with Mr Macpherson's translation. These pieces, or fragments, are as follows :

" *The description of Cuchullin's chariot*—'Fingal,' Book I., page 11.

* H. S. R., App., p. 176.　　　　† Id., p. 9.

"The rehearsers are John Macdonald of Breackish, in Strath, Isle of Skye, gentleman; Martin Macgilvray, tenant in Sleat; and Allan Macaskle, farmer in Glenelg.

"*The episode relating to Faineasolis* — 'Fingal,' Book III., page 45.

"The rehearsers are, among others, John Macdonald of Breackish, in Strath; Alexander Macdonald, merchant in Sleat; John Down, cowherd there; and John Maclean, carpenter in the parish of Strath.

"*The actions of Ossian at the Lake of Lego, and his courtship of Everallin*—'Fingal,' Book IV., page 50.

"The rehearsers are Alexander Macdonald, merchant in Sleat; Nicol Mackenzie, in the parish of Strath, gentleman; and Ewan Macpherson, schoolmaster in Glenelg.

"*Fingal's combat with the King of Lochlin*—'Fingal,' Book V., page 62.

"The rehearsers, Alexander Macdonald, merchant in Sleat; Donald Robertson, tenant there; and Nicol Mackenzie, just mentioned, together with many more.

"*The Battle of Lora*, page 111.

"The rehearsers are Alexander Macdonald, merchant in Sleat; John Maclean, carpenter in Strath; and Neil Mackinnon, farmer there.

"*Darthula*, page 155.

"The rehearsers are Alexander Morison, in the parish of Durnish, gentleman; Ewen Macpherson, schoolmaster in Glenelg; and John Down, cowherd in Sleat.

"*The combat between Oscar and Ullin*, in the Fragments.

"The rehearsers are John Macdonald of Breackish,

THE POEMS OF OSSIAN.

Alexander Morison, and John Down—all three above mentioned.

" *The Lamentation of Dargo*—sung by thousands in the Isles.

" These are all the pieces of Ossian's poems, as published by Mr Macpherson, known to the rehearsers whom I have had occasion to consult. Had it been in my power to have travelled farther than through my parish and that next to it, I have reason to believe that I would easily have found many more such on record in the memories of others who have a taste for our old Gaelic compositions. The rehearsers whom I had occasion to consult have repeated in my hearing several other poems which have much of the spirit and character of Ossian."

The Rev. Mr M'Neill, minister of Hovemore, in Uist, writing in answer to Dr Blair, of date 23d December 1763, says : *

" Mr Macdonald of Demisdale, a parishioner of mine, rehearsed from memory before me some passages which agreed exactly with the translation, viz. :

" *The terms of peace proposed by Morla in Swaran's name to Cuchullin*—' Fingal,' Book II., page 26.

" Likewise Fingal's orders for raising his standards, his orders to his chiefs before the battle, the chiefs' resolutions thereupon of fighting each of them a Lochlin chief, contained in pages 57 and 58 of ' Fingal,' Book IV.

" Also the single combat between Fingal and Swaran, which in the original is expressed in the strongest lan-

* H. S. R., App., p. 18.

guage, and perfectly agreed with the translation, which
is very just here and in all other places I had occasion
to compare. The passage alluded to is 'Fingal,' Book
V., page 62."

"Archibald M'Lellan, likewise a parishioner of mine,
who repeated before me in Gaelic Ossian's account of
his own courtship of Everallin at the Lake of Lego,
without any material variation from the translation—
'Fingal,' Book IV., pages 40, 50, and 51.

"Neil M'Murich, a native of this county, repeated
before me the whole of the poem of *Darthula*, or *Clan-
usnoch*, with few variations from the translation."

Lieutenant Duncan MacNicol, late of the 88th
Regiment, writes to the Rev. Alexander Macaulay,
January 1764 : *

"I was from home when yours of the 17th ult. came
to this place (Sock-rock, in Glenorchy), but since my
return I have been at some pains to examine severals
in this country about Ossian's poems, and have found
out as follows :

"'Fingal,' Book III., page 45, 'Oscar, I was young
like thee when lovely *Faineasollis*,' &c., to the end of
the Third Book.

"'Fingal,' Book IV., page 50, '*Eight were the heroes
of Ossian*,' &c., mostly word for word to page 58, or the
end of the Fourth Book.

"The story of *Orla* in the beginning of the Fifth
Book to page 71.

"'Then Gaul and Ossian sat on the green bank of
Lubar.'

" The Battle of *Lora*, nearly.

" *Darthula*, page 155, pretty well to the end of page 171.

" *Temora*, much the same, page 172 to the end of page 190.

" *Carric-Thura*, page 207, ' Who can reach the source of thy race, O'Connal,' &c., till you come to the passage that begins thus—' Dire was the clang of their steel.'

" Those that know most about the history of Ossian and his poems in this country are now *no more :* formerly I might, I daresay, make out a great deal more among them. At this very day there are many in this country, who can neither read nor write, that can repeat poems composed by Ossian, at least pretty much in the same strain, which would make a larger volume if they were all gathered together than that which Mr Macpherson has given to the public."

The Rev. Donald Macleod, minister of Glenelg, writing to Dr Blair, of date 26th March 1764, says : *

" It was in my house that Mr Macpherson got the description of Cuchullin's horses and car in ' Fingal,' Book I., page 11, from Allan MacCaskle, schoolmaster, and Rory Macleod, both of this glen. He has not taken in the whole of the description, and his translation of it, spirited as far as it goes, falls so far short of the original in the picture it exhibits of Cuchullin's horses and car, their harness, trappings, &c., that in none of his translations is the inequality of Macpherson's genius to that of Ossian so very conspicuous.

" *The Battle of Lena* in ' Fingal,' Book II., is still

* H S. R., App., p. 28.

preserved by tradition in this country; but with this variation, that the proposal of giving up his wife and dog in page 26, as the only condition on which peace would be granted, was made by Magnus, King of Lochlin, to Fingal, and not by Swaran to Cuchullin.

"I have heard the poem in Book III., relating Fingal's voyage to Lochlin, the snares laid for him by Starno, death of Agandecca, how for his cruelty and perfidiousness he took immediate revenge on Starno, when, page 38, he eyed his valiant chiefs—'his valiant chiefs took arms.'

"The poem in Book IV. is handed down pretty entire in this country, in which each of Fingal's chiefs singles out the chief among the enemy he was to fight, leaving to Fingal the honour of engaging the King of Lochlin.

"The description of the sunbeam, Fingal's standard, does not come up to the beauty and spirit of the original. Along with that of the sunbeam, there is in the original a particular description of the standards of the seven principal chiefs of Fingal, which are so inimitably beautiful that I cannot imagine how Macpherson has omitted them in his translation.

"We have the poem containing the battle of Lochlego, and a good part of that relating to the war of Inisthona in page 104.

"It would take up too much room, and I think it is not necessary that I go through all the poems in the collection of which we have pieces joined to other poems, and sometimes parts of two or three poems thrown together into one.

"Mr Macpherson, in his journey through the Highlands, put it upon me to look out for the poem called *Cath, or the Battle of Benedin*. I have since got it, but not till after the book was published. The battle is the most memorable of Fingal's exploits, and I humbly think the poem is the most finished of Ossian's works.

"One thing I am sorry for, his having omitted the description which Ossian gives of Fingal's ships, their sails, masts, and rigging, their extraordinary feats in sailing, the skill and dexterity of his men in working them, and their intrepidity in the greatest storms, of which he gives the most striking description. I can account for it in no other way than his having been born in Badenoch, one of the most inland parts of this kingdom, where, not having access to, he was unacquainted with that kind of imagery ; he did not, therefore, perhaps understand the original poems."

Dr Adam Ferguson, writing from Hallyards, near Peebles, 26th March 1798, says :[*]

"In answer to the first query, the Committee will please to know that about the year 1740 I heard John Fleming, a taylor, who, in the manner of the country, worked with journeymen at my father's house, repeat, in a kind of chiming measure, heroic strains relating to an arrival or landing of an host, and a subsequent battle, with a single combat of two chiefs. This I took down in writing and kept for some time, but was not in possession of when Mr Macpherson's publications appeared. I had no doubt, however, in recognising the

* H. S. R., App., p. 63.

same passage in the arrival of Swarran and the single combat with Cuthullin in Macpherson's translation of 'Fingal.'

"The few words I can recall are, first, in relation to the hosts engaged—

" ' Iomma colan, iomma skia,
    Iomma tria is lurigh gharibh;'

and in relation to the chiefs who grappled, and in whose struggle—

" ' Bha cloghin agus talamh trom
    Moscle fo bhonn an cos.'

"I have at different times heard other scraps or fragments repeated, but the principal use I made of them was to tell my friend and companion at college, Mr John Home, that there were such relics of ancient poetry in the Highlands, *and which led him to the inquiries which produced Mr Macpherson's communications.*"

The Rev. Mr M'Diarmid of Weem, in his letter to Mr Mackenzie, of date 9th April 1801, enclosing copy of Ossian's Address to the Sun, says :*

"As I have not a copy of Mr Macpherson's translation by me I could not compare it with the original, nor point out wherein he has departed from it. Mr Mackenzie will easily see that by comparing his translation with mine. I got the copy of these poems about thirty years ago from an old man in Glenlyon. I took it and several fragments, now, I fear, irrecoverably lost,

* H. S. R., p. 71.

from the man's mouth ; he had learnt them in his youth from people in the same glen, which must have been long before Mr Macpherson was born."

Sir John Macpherson, writing from Laurieston to Dr Blair, of date 4th February 1763, when sending some Ossianic poems *in Gaelic verse*, says : *

" I do myself the pleasure of presenting you with a few specimens of Ossian in his native dress. I could have drawn out many other pieces of greater length, and of more merit, but the enclosed may satisfy Mr Percy's curiosity ; and it is unnecessary to trouble you with more of the original at present, as you can at any time command all my collection.

" Those poems that I have selected had each a particular title to regard.

" Ossian's courtship of Everallin is a short and entire story. It is a monument of the simplicity and dignity with which the courtships of princes were carried on in the poet's days.

" The Address to the Evening Star claimed attention on account of its inimitable beauty *and harmonious versification*. The original of this piece suffered even in the hands of Mr Macpherson, though he has shown himself inferior to no translator. The copy or edition which he had of this poem is very different from mine ; I imagine it will in that respect be agreeable to Mr Percy. The gentlemen who gave it to me copied it from an old MS. which Mr Macpherson had no access to peruse before his ' Fingal ' came abroad.

* H. S. R., App., p. 1.

" *Ullin's* war-song will, I hope, give satisfaction, as
it is a singular species of poetry, and refers to a very
ancient custom. The gentleman who gave me this
valuable piece of antiquity told me that he had formerly
given Mr Macpherson a copy of it at full length.

" All that can be said of my translation of these
pieces is, that it is extremely literal, and that it was
not attempted to imitate the conciseness and strength
of the original.

" I can likewise assure you, upon my honour, that
I never received any of these originals from Mr Macpherson, nor took the least assistance from his translation. This was so far from being the case, that after
I had done my translation and compared it with his, I
was obliged to reject several proper phrases only because
he had used them.

" If you forward these specimens to Mr Percy, he
certainly will make the requisite allowances for the
difference of copies. Others to whom he will, perhaps,
show them, and who are less known to the manner in
which our ancient poetry was preserved, shall not be
equally candid. But after you have convinced men of
the nicest taste in Europe, *it would be a mistake in
any one to endeavour to convince those who have not
the power of believing, or the good taste to discover
the genuineness and antiquity of any work from the
turn of its composition.*"

It should be borne in mind that these recitations of
the originals of Ossian were in Gaelic *verse*, and by
persons many of whom were quite illiterate; and also
that they were made upwards of forty years before the

originals collected by Mr Macpherson were given to the public by his executors.

It is plain from the above how much Mr Macpherson was indebted to oral recitation for the collection of Ossianic poetry made by him.

Having shown the mode in which Mr Macpherson made his collection, let us now advert to confirmation derived from other sources as to the authenticity of what he has given to the public.

That Mr Macpherson was the largest collector of Gaelic poetry is not to be wondered at, for he travelled over a great portion of the Highlands, and bestowed considerable labour and research in recovering the remains of ancient Gaelic poetry, not only personally, but also through his friends ; whereas other collectors generally confined themselves to the neighbourhood of their own localities, and were content to note only what came incidentally to their notice.

One of the earliest of these independent collections was that of the Dean of Lismore, recently brought to notice. It was written between 1512 and 1529, and is found to contain several of the poems translated by Macpherson ; but these poems having been obtained from oral recitation, they vary somewhat in expression from the versions obtained by Macpherson, though the incidents are the same. Among these we may mention 'The Death of Oscar,' at the battle of Gaura, of which there are two editions, one at page 35 and the other at page 49 of Dr M'Lauchlan's translation, similar to 'The Death of Oscar' as given by Macpherson at the

same battle in the beginning of 'Temora.'   We quote
from page 49 :

> " It would be hard to tell,
>   'Twould be a heavy task,
>   To number all that fell
>   Slain by the arms of Oscar.
>   No swifter is a cataract,
>   Or hawk in sweeping stoop,
>   Or rapids rushing fast,
>   Than in that fight was Oscar.
>   You saw him last of all,
>   Like leaves in windy weather,
>   Or like a noble aspen
>   When hewers strike its stem.
>   When Erin's king he saw
>   Still living 'midst the fight,
>   Oscar swift approached him
>   As waves break on the strand.
>   When Cairbar this observed
>   He shook his hungry spear
>   And through him drove its point,
>   Chiefest of all our griefs !
>   Yet Oscar did not quail
>   But made for Erin's king,
>   With force he aimed a blow
>   And smote him with his sword.
>   Then Art Mac Cairbar fell,
>   Struck with the second blow.
>   So it was that Oscar perished
>   With glory as a king.

Pages 38, 39.

" His shattered shield beside him ;
  While his hand still grasped his sword
  His precious blood on every side
  Flowed swiftly through his harness.

Page 41.

" Sad it is, my brave Oscar,
  Thou good son of my son :
  After thee I'm but feeble.
  And after Erin's brave Feinn
  The heavy curse of Art Aenir
  Is on us to our great grief ;
  From the East it me pursued,
  Following me along the field.
  Farewell to battle and to fame.

" His own son did no man mourn,
  Nor did mourn his brother ;
  As they saw how lay my son,
  All did mourn for Oscar.

" When Oscar had heard Finn's wail,
  Convulsive pangs did him seize ;
  Both of his hands he stretched forth,
  And his soft fair eyelid fell.
  From us then Finn turned away
  And shed many bitter tears,
  But for Oscar and for Bran
  Never did he shed a tear.

" Then raised we the noble Oscar
Aloft on the shafts of our spears ;
To a fair green knoll we bore him
That we his dress might remove :
Of his body one hand's breadth
Was not whole down from his hair
Till you reached the sole of his foot."

There is also the poem of *Fainesolis* or 'The Sun-beam,' given at page 20 of the Dean of Lismore's collection, which is introduced by way of episode by Macpherson under the name of ' *The Maid of Craca*,' in the 4th book of ' Fingal.'

Also the poem of *Conloch* at page 50, which is the ' *Carthon* ' of Macpherson.

From the intercourse between the west coast of Scotland and Ireland, which might be considered one country, having a community of manners and language, as well as the closest political connection, the scenes described in some of these poems were of common interest to both nations. That they were known in both countries, appears from various sources. In the collection published by Miss Brooke, entitled ' Reliques of Irish Poetry,' in 1789, the first is a description of the Battle of Gaura, under the title of Magnus the Great; the second, *Fainesolis*, under the title of *Moira Borb ;* and the third bears the same name of *Conloch* as that above mentioned. But in the poem of Magnus *there is no mention of the death of Oscar.*

The tragical story of *Darthula* and of three sons of Usnoch—Naos, Ainle, and Arden—is contained in the

Glenmasen MS. in the Advocates' Library at Edinburgh,
but differs somewhat from that published by Mr Macpherson. The MS. is dated 1238. The following is
the lament of Darthula over Alban taken from that
manuscript, and not given by Mr Macpherson. The
scenery is in Argyllshire. *Literal translation:*

"Beloved land, that Eastern land,
Alba with its wonders,
O that I might not depart from it,
But that I go with Naise.

"Beloved is Dunfidhgha and Dun Finn,
Beloved the Dun above them,
Beloved is Innisdraighende,
And beloved Suibhne.

"Coillchuan! O Coillchuan!
Where Ainnle would, alas! resort;
Too short I deem was then my stay,
With Ainnle in Oirir Alban.

"Glenlaidhe! O Glenlaidhe!
I use to sleep by its soothing murmur;
Fish and flesh of wild boar and badger
Was my repast in Glenlaidhe.

"Glenmassan! O Glenmassan!
High its herbs, fair its boughs,
Solitary was the place of our repose
On grassy Invermassan.

" Gleneitche ! O Gleneitche !
There was raised my earliest home ;
Beautiful its woods on rising
When the sun struck on Gleneitche.

" Glen Urchain ! O Glen Urchain !
It was the straight glen of smooth ridges ;
Not more joyful was a man of his age,
Than Naoise in Glen Urchain.

" Glenduruadh ! O Glenduruadh !
My love each man of its inheritance ;
Sweet the voice of the cuckoo on bending bough
On the hill above Glenduruadh.

" Beloved is Draighen and its sounding shore,
Beloved the water o'er pure sand ;
O that I might not depart from the east
But that I go with my beloved."

Mr Jerome Stone, a schoolmaster at Dunkeld, in Perthshire, commenced a collection of ancient Gaelic poetry, and published a translation of one of the poems, *Bas Fhraoich*, in the 'Scots Magazine' in 1756, under the name of 'Albin and the Daughter of Mey;' but having died at an early age, his collection was not completed. This poem is also in the Dean of Lismore's collection.

The next collection of importance is that of Mr Duncan Kennedy, a schoolmaster at Craignish, in Argyllshire, which was begun in 1774 and completed in 1785. It consists of upwards of twenty pieces, the reciters of which are named by him, and contains a number of the poems given by the Dean of Lismore, several of those given by Miss Brooke, also the *Battle of Lora* given by Macpherson, and the poem of *Conloch*, where Conal is represented as sending for Cuchullin to oppose the victorious stranger, whose progress to the combat is described with the same sublime and terrible imagery which is given in Macpherson's translation of *The Death of Cuchullin*. The subject of this passage is remarkable, as the 'Spirit of Loda' has been a cause of dispute among the inquirers into the authenticity of the poems of Ossian. It is much admired in the original, and is therefore inserted here, with a translation :

> " Ruidh e fiar le tartar uamhan,
>   'S fuaimneach arm mar spiorad Lodda,
>   Sgaoile goiraig is crith chatha
>   Fea an rathaid gu grad chòrag.
>   Mar mhile tonn a beacaich
>   In stoirm citidh re slios carraige,
>   B'amhail fuaim arm 'f a luirich,
>   'S ar a ghnuis bha dulachd catha.
>   Bha claidheamh liobhaidh a dealra
>   Togt' anàird in laimh a churaidh,
>   Is na gaotha frannor ag gluasad
>   A chiabh ar snua frotha buinne.
>   Na cnuic ar gach taobh dhe chrithich,—
>   Chlisg ant shlighe fu a chosan,
>   Las a shuilean, dhat a chridhe,
>   B'aufheilidh a chith is a choltas."

" He rushed west with terror in his tread,
  In the sound of his arms like the spirit of Loda
  When he scatters dismay and panic fear
  In the path of sudden conflict.
  As a thousand waves which roar
  In the wrath of the storm against a rock,
  Such was the sound of his arms and mail
  While the gloom of battle spread over his counte-
      nance;
  His polished sword gleamed uplifted
  In the hand of the champion ;
  While the rustling winds tossed his locks
  Like the foam of a rapid stream.
  The little hills quaked around him,
  The path shook under his steps,
  His eyes flamed, his heart swelled—
  Awful was the storm of his face."

About the year 1780, Mr John Clark, land-surveyor
in Badenoch, published translations of ancient Gaelic
poetry. The next collector of importance was the Rev.
Dr John Smith, minister of Kilbrandon, in Argyllshire,
who in 1780 published the translations of fourteen
Gaelic poems collected by him, all of them of great
merit, and some as beautiful as any published by Macpherson. The originals were published in 1787, and
extend to about 4000 lines. In these poems are to be
found, not only the same strain of high and impassioned
poetry, but also the same delicacy and refinement of
sentiment which form so remarkable a feature in
the poems translated by Macpherson. In particular

we would mention *Tiomna Ghuill* or 'The Death of
Gaul.' The opening of the poem is in that spirit of
melancholy which Ossian indulges when he recalls
the deeds of the heroes of his race.

" Is not the silence of night mournful,
  While she spreads her dark clouds over the vales ?
  Sleep has descended on the youth of the chase,
  Upon the heath, his dog resting against his knee.
  The children of the mountains he pursues
  In his dream, while his sleep is forsaking him.
  Sleep, ye children of fatigue,
  While each star but ascends the height.
  Sleep, swift dog of the course,
  Ossian will not interrupt your slumbers.
  I am watching alone :
  Soothing to me is the gloom of night,
  While I travel from dell to dell,
  Without hope of morning or dawn.
  Spare thy light, O Sun !
  And do not consume so fast thy torches :
  Like the King of the Fingalians, generous is thy
      soul,
  But thy liberality will hereafter fail—
  Spare the torches of thousand flames
  In thy blue hall, when thou goest
  Under the dusky gates to sleep
  Beneath the darkened skirt of the western sky—
  Spare them, before they leave thee alone,
  As I am, without a person to share my fondness—
  Spare them, since there is not a hero to view

The blue flame of the beautiful torches.
Caothan of the joyful lights,
Thy torches are now darkened ;
Like an oak which has quickly faded,
Thy dwellings and their people have failed.
East or west, on the face of thy mountain,
There is not found of one of them but the ruin
In *Seallama*,* in *Taura* or *Tigh-mo-ri* ; *
There is no shell, nor song, nor harp ;
They are all become green mounds,
And their stones in their own meadows.
The stranger will not perceive from the desert
Any of them showing its head through the cloud.
   " And thou, Seallama, house of my delight !
Is this heap thine old ruin ?
Where now grows the thistle, the heath, and the rank
      grass,
Mourning under the drops of night ?
Around my grey locks
The solitary owl flutters,
And the roe starts from her bed
Without fearing the mournful Ossian.
   " Roe of the hollow cairns,
Where dwelt Oscar and Fion,
I will not do thee any hurt ;
Never shalt thou be wounded by my dart.
To the top of Seallama I stretch my hand—
The dwelling has no cover but sky.
I search for the broad shield below.
The top of my spear has struck its boss—

* The Selma and Temora of Macpherson.

Sounding boss of battles !
Gladdening to me is thy sound ;
It awakes the days that have passed,
And, in spite of age, my soul bounds."

The only other collector we shall notice was the
Rev. Alexander Irvine of Little Dunkeld, who, when a
missionary in Rannoch (a very remote part of the
country), made a collection of Ossianic poems, many of
which are the same as those published by Macpherson,
but varied in expression by the different reciters. These
poems were collected between the years 1801 and
1805, and the name of each reciter, and the date of
the recitation, is particularly mentioned. This collection is in the possession of the Irvine family, in the
handwriting of the collector, and has never been published.

The various collections now enumerated were made
from the oral recitations of uneducated persons, who
recited in Gaelic verse, and at a period long previous to
1807, the date when the extant portion of the Gaelic
versions that were in the possession of Macpherson
was published by the Highland Society. They could
not therefore have been derived from the latter source.
Yet we find that many of the poems contained in these
several independent collections are not only substan-
tially the same, but likewise closely resemble poems
contained in the portion that has been recovered and
published of the Gaelic poems collected by Macpherson, and embodied by him in the English Ossian which
he published in the form of an epic. Among these

arc the following, which are about the most beautiful parts of Ossian, and on that account have probably been longest cherished in recitation :

1. The description of *Cuchullin's* chariot—'Fingal,' Book I.
2. The Battle of *Lena*—'Fingal,' Book II.
3. The episode of *Fainesolis* — 'Fingal,' Book III.
4. Fingal's voyage to *Lochlin*. The snares laid for him by Starno, and the death of *Agandecca*—'Fingal,' Book III.
5. The actions of Ossian at the Lake of *Lego*, and his courtship of Everallin — 'Fingal,' Book IV.
6. The description of the opening of the battle. The raising of the standards. The orders to the chiefs. Their resolutions of fighting each a chief ; and so to the end of Book IV.
7. Fingal's combat with *Swaran*—'Fingal,' Book V.
8. The episode of *Orla*—Book V.
9. A portion of the latter part of this book— "Then Gaul and Ossian sat with Swaran on the green banks of *Lubar*"—Book V.
10. The battle of *Lora*.
11. *Conlath*, or the war of Inisthona.
12. *Carthon*, similar to Conloch, and in particular the Address to the Sun.
13. The death of *Cuthullin*, or the battle of *Lochlego*.
14. *Darthula*.

15. Address to the sun in *Carric - Thura*, and a small portion towards the end of the poem.
16. Part of *Berrathon*.
17. Address to the Evening Star, in *the Song of Selma*.
18. Part of *Temora*.
19. The combat between *Oscar* and *Ullin* in the 'Fragments.'
20. *Ullin's war-song.*
21. The lamentation of *Dargos*' spouse.

We know not with certainty how many Gaelic poems were collected by Macpherson which are not comprehended in his collection as published, but it is to be inferred from the number of the manuscripts recovered by him, and the oral recitations collected by him, that he was in possession of a much larger number of poems, and more perfect versions of them, than were collected by those that followed him.

That the Gaelic poems which he directed to be published were obtained by him in the form in which they now appear, and were neither translations from the English, nor modern compositions of his own or of any one connected with him, is evident from what has been already stated, and is proved by the direct testimony of those who assisted in their collection and translation. We have Mr Lachlan Macpherson of Strathmashie, who says,—" I took down from oral tradition, and transcribed from old manuscripts, by far the greatest part of these pieces he has published. I have carefully compared the translation with the copies of the originals in my hands, and find it amazingly literal."

We have also Ewan Macpherson, who was employed with James Macpherson for weeks in taking down these poems from recitation :* "That some time subsequent to the above excursion, he met Mr Macpherson at Edinburgh, and was presented by him with a copy of 'Fingal': That he recollects to have read a part of it, and to have been then of opinion, as far as he could recollect the substance of the original, that this translation was well executed."

We have also the testimony of Captain Morison, who says,† "That he got the Address to the Sun among Mr Macpherson's original papers, when transcribing fairly for him from these original papers (either collected by himself or transmitted by his Highland friends), as it stood in the poem of '*Carthon*,' afterwards translated and published.

"Admits he had much merit in collecting, arranging, and translating; but that he was no great poet, nor thoroughly conversant in Gaelic literature; so far from composing such poems as were translated, that he assisted him often in understanding some words, and suggested some improvements; that he could as well compose the Prophecies of Isaiah, or create the island of Skye, as compose a poem like one of Ossian's; that there are many other such poems which Macpherson did not collect, and collected some which he did not translate, but made choice with proper taste."

Next to those who were engaged in assisting Mac-

pherson in his collections, stood, in point of knowledge,
Dr Blair; and he, writing to Mr Mackenzie on the
20th December 1797, says :* "Scepticism has indeed
been entertained by many how far his work, supposing
it to be no imposture on the whole, could be relied
upon as an accurate and faithful translation of his
Gaelic originals? That in some of the longer works
he may have combined and brought together some
pieces which he found scattered and broken ; and that,
in comparing the different copies which he frequently
found of the same poem, either in manuscript or by
rehearsal, he selected from them all such as he thought
the best readings, I make no doubt, nor did he himself
seek to disown it. I also think it probable that he
may have left out some rudenesses and extravagances
which he might occasionally find in the old Gaelic
songs. But, after all the inquiries I have been at pains
to make, I can find no ground to suspect that his devia-
tions from the original text were at all considerable, or
his interpolations any more than what were simply necessary to connect together pieces of one whole which he
found disjointed. That his work, as it stands, exhibits
a genuine authentic view of ancient Gaelic poetry, I
am as firmly persuaded as I can be of anything."

The view taken by Dr Blair of the mode of arrange-
ment of the pieces collected by Macpherson, is to a
certain extent corroborated by Macpherson himself in
his letter to Mr M'Lagan, where he says : " I have met
with a number of old manuscripts in my travels ; the
poetical part of them I have endeavoured to secure.

* H. S. R., App., p. 61.

"Your collection, I am informed, is pure, as you have taken pains to restore the style."

Again, in the preface to '*Temora*,' he says: "By means of my friends I have since collected all the broken fragments of '*Temora*' that I formerly wanted; and the story of the poem, which was accurately preserved by many, enabled me to reduce it into that order in which it now appears. The title of epic was imposed on the poem by myself.

"The reader will find some alterations in the style of this book. These are drawn from more correct copies of the original, which came to my hands since the former publication. As the most part of the poem is delivered down by tradition, the style is sometimes various and interpolated. After comparing the different readings, I always made choice of that which agreed best with the spirit of the context."

This is an accurate account of the collection and publication of the poems of Ossian by Macpherson, and contains nearly all that is known on the subject.

Let us now see who his assailants were, and what were their arguments.

The first was the celebrated Dr Samuel Johnson, whose word was at that time law on all literary matters. He at once denounced Macpherson as an impostor, and his work a fiction. In 1773 he undertook a journey to the Highlands with Mr Boswell, but neither of them being acquainted with the Gaelic language, they could hold no communication with those who could recite Ossian's poems. Johnson returned with his opinion unchanged, and soon afterwards published his Tour,

in which he spoke of Macpherson and his works in the
most offensive manner. He says :*

"I suppose my opinion of the poems of Ossian is
already discovered. *I believe they never existed in
any other form than that which we have seen.* The
editor, or author, never could show the original, nor
can it be shown by any other. To revenge reasonable
incredulity by refusing evidence is a degree of insolence
with which the world is not yet acquainted, and stub-
born audacity is the last refuge of guilt. It would be
easy to show it if he had it ; but whence could it be
had? It is too long to be remembered, *and the language formerly had nothing written.* He has doubt-
less inserted names that circulate in popular stories,
and may have translated some wandering ballads, if
any can be found; and the names of some of the images
being recollected, make an inaccurate auditor imagine,
by the help of Caledonian bigotry, that he has formerly
heard the whole.

"It is said that some men of integrity profess to
have heard parts of it, but they all heard them when
they were boys, *and it was never said that any of
them could recite six lines.*

"The Scots have something to plead for their easy
reception of an improbable fiction ; they are seduced by
their fondness for their supposed ancestors. A Scotch-
man must be a very sturdy moralist who does not love
Scotland better than truth ; he will always love it
better than inquiry, and, if falsehood flatters his vanity,
will not be very diligent to detect it."

* See Boswell's Johnson, 6th ed., vol. ii., p. 273.

This rude attack roused Macpherson, and drew him forth from the silence which he had hitherto observed. He wrote to Johnson, and placed his original manuscripts in Mr Becket the London bookseller's shop, intimating by advertisement in the newspapers that he had done so. He then called upon Johnson to retract his accusations; and on his refusing to do so, he sent him a message by his friend Mr William Duncan, of Brunswick Square, London, and on Johnson's declining to give satisfaction, threatened to chastise him.* It is to be regretted that we have not Macpherson's letters to Johnson, but from Johnson's letters, as given by his biographer, Mr Boswell, we have enough to substantiate the accuracy of the above statement. It is further said that Johnson provided himself with a large stick for the purpose of self-defence; but as he threatened legal proceedings, Macpherson did not carry out his intention.

That he placed the originals of Ossian in Becket's shop there is abundant evidence. Dr Blair says :† "These doubts his temper led him to disdain, perhaps to disdain too much. So far, however, he endeavoured to give satisfaction to the public, that for some months he left all the originals of his translation in Becket the bookseller's shop, and intimated by advertisement in the newspapers that he had done so." And Sir John Sinclair, who lived a great portion of the year in London, and was intimate with Macpherson, says, in his dissertation prefixed to the Gaelic Ossian, that he placed in Becket's shop not only all the original manuscripts,

* See dissertation by Sir John Sinclair, App., p. 220.
† H. S. R., App., p. 59.

but the extracts made from them by himself and his friends.

Boswell, having heard of the altercation which had taken place betwixt Johnson and Macpherson, writes to Johnson from Edinburgh on the 2d February 1775 :*

"As to Macpherson, I am anxious to have from yourself a full and pointed account of what has passed between you and him. It is confidently told here that before your book came out he sent to you to let you know that he understood you meant to deny the authenticity of Ossian's poems; that the originals were in his possession; that you might have inspection of them, and might take the evidence of people skilled in the Erse language; and that he hoped, after this fair offer, you would not be so uncandid as to assert that he had refused reasonable proof. That you paid no regard to this message, but published your strong attack upon him ; and then he wrote a letter to you in such terms as he thought suited to one who had not acted as a man of veracity.

"You may believe it gives me pain to hear your conduct represented as unfavourable, while I can only deny what is said on the ground that your character refutes it, without having any information to oppose· Let me, I beg it of you, be furnished with a sufficient answer to any calumny upon this occasion."

Johnson answers this letter on the 7th February 1775 as follows : †

* See Boswell's Johnson, 6th ed., vol. ii. p. 308.
† Boswell, vol. ii. p. 310.

"I am surprised that, knowing as you do the disposition of your countrymen to tell lies in favour of each other, you can be at all affected by any reports that circulate among them. Macpherson never in his life offered me a sight of any original, or of any evidence of any kind, but thought only of intimidating me by noise and threats, till my last answer—that I would not be deterred from detecting what I thought a cheat by the menaces of a ruffian—put an end to our correspondence.

"The state of the question is this: He and Dr Blair, whom I consider deceived, say that he copied the poem from old manuscripts. His copies, if he had them, and I believe him to have none, are nothing—where are the manuscripts? They can be shown if they exist, but they were never shown. *De non existentibus et non apparentibus*, says our law, *eadem est ratio*. No man has a claim to credit upon his word when better evidence, if he had it, may be easily produced. But, so far as we can find, the Erse language was never written till very lately for the purposes of religion. A nation that cannot write, or a language that was never written, has no manuscripts.

"But whatever he has, he never offered to show. If old manuscripts should now be mentioned, I should, unless there were more evidence than can be easily had, suppose them another proof of Scotch conspiracy in national falsehood."

A most uncandid letter, as will be seen by reference to Boswell's letter to Johnson on 27th of the previous month, in which he asked,—

" What does Becket mean by the originals of 'Fingal' and other poems of Ossian, which he advertises to have lain in his shop ?" *

Now here we have it under Boswell's hand that while Johnson was asserting that Macpherson had no originals, and that he had never offered to show them, he was at that very time aware where they were placed, and had been invited by advertisement to see them. But in the latter part of his letter Johnson betrays his knowledge of the fact, for he says that *if* old manuscripts *should now be mentioned*, he should suppose them another proof of Scotch conspiracy in national falsehood. Does this show the great love of " truth " and of " inquiry " which he so ostentatiously professes, and which he wishes the public to believe belongs exclusively to himself ? It is to be regretted that Macpherson's letter to Johnson has not been preserved, for it might have thrown more light on this controversy, but Boswell gives the following, dictated to him by Johnson, as being the purport of the reply he had made :

" I received your foolish and impudent letter. Any violence offered me I shall do my best to repel, and what I cannot do for myself the law shall do for me. I hope I shall never be deterred from detecting what I think a cheat by the menaces of a ruffian.

" What would you have me retract ? I thought your book an imposture, and I think it an imposture still. For this opinion I have given my reasons to the public, which I dare you to refute. Your rage I defy.

* Boswell, 6th ed., vol. ii. p. 310.

Your abilities, since your Homer, are not so formidable, and what I hear of your morals inclines me to pay regard, not to what you shall say, but to what you shall prove. You may print this if you will."

In these letters there is not only a want of fairness, but also a perversion or utter ignorance of fact. Johnson says that Gaelic was never, till lately, a written language. Now, as before stated, although many manuscripts have no doubt been lost, there are still some to be found in private collections, and there are at this moment no fewer than 65 in the Advocates' Library at Edinburgh, some of which are as old as the eleventh century; and in Ireland they greatly exceed this number. In the next place, he says that no one in the Highlands could repeat six lines of Ossianic poetry. Ample evidence has been produced to refute that statement. Yet the great authority quoted to this day against the authenticity of Ossian's poems is Dr Johnson, which tends to prove how few have studied the matter for themselves. Not only is the idea that a whole nation could be capable of contributing to the forgery of these manuscripts an extravagant absurdity, but the resort to such a rabid calumny as a reason for not listening to evidence indicates a state of moral blindness incompatible with dispassionate judgment.

The next assailant of Macpherson was Mr Malcolm Laing, an Edinburgh barrister, and an Orkney proprietor, who entered on his task with all the dogmatism of Johnson and the anti-Celtic antipathy of his countrymen. In 1805 he republished Macpherson's

translation with numerous notes, in which he ran-
sacked all the authors, ancient and modern, for parallel
passages to those in Macpherson's Ossian. This species
of criticism has long been looked upon with distrust; for
as similes are for the most part taken from natural
objects, there must to a certain extent be a correspondence between different authors, though without any
plagiarism. How far Mr Laing's analogies are fair
and just will be seen presently. But, in the first place,
let us see how far his deductions are authorised by his
premises. The *animus* with which Mr Laing set about
his task may be gathered from the following:* "His
private character may well be spared; and it is sufficient
to observe that his morals were not such as to refute
the charge which I have made, that, with a genius truly
poetical, he was one of the first literary impostors in
modern times." This is truly Johnsonian, and rather
a begging of the question.

Mr Laing says that the words given by Dr Ferguson
of the single combat of Swaran and Cuthullin is not
in Ossian, but is to be found in the Irish ballad of Fingal and Magnus. On what authority does he make
this statement? Miss Brooke publishes the ballad of
Magnus, but it is not there.

Mr Laing founds on the similarity of the description
of Fingal's Standard by Macpherson, and that in the
poem of Magnus, as a proof of Macpherson's imposture,
while, in fact, it is evidence of the authenticity of the
Ossianic poems, and of Laing's own ignorance of material facts. For Macpherson was never in Ireland, and

* See addition to sketch of Macpherson's life in Laing's preface.

could not have seen the original of the poem of Magnus till published by Miss Brooke with a translation in 1789, whereas Macpherson's translation appeared in 1761. *The Battle of Gaura*, which is the subject of the poems of Fingal and of Magnus, was fought in Ulster by the forces of Cuthullin and Fingal against Swaran ; and their similarity only proves that these poems, though differing in version, were common to the traditions of both countries.

In regard to the fragments given to Mr Home by Macpherson, at Moffat in 1759, Mr Laing says : " In a day or two he produced the fragment on the death of Oscar, which of all others is the most demonstratively a forgery, and which Macpherson himself was obliged afterwards to appropriate to another Oscar, the son of Caruth. When the very first poem produced by Macpherson is an almost avowed fabrication, it is evident that, on finding the genuine Erse ballads unfit for translation, he could not resist the temptation to vindicate that neglected merit of which he was conscious by submitting *his own poetry*, which the public had hitherto overlooked, to a distinguished judge as a relic of antiquity."

This is a fair specimen of Mr Laing's species of criticism. It will be remembered that when Macpherson met Mr Home at Moffat accidentally in 1759, he was only twenty-one years of age. Mr Home having heard from Dr A. Ferguson, himself a Highlander, that there were remains of ancient Gaelic poetry in the Highlands, approached Macpherson on the subject; and on learning that he had some fragments in his possession which he had taken down from recitation, he requested him to translate two of them, which Macpherson did, after some reluctance, fearing that a prose translation would not do justice to the original; but eventually he did translate them into English prose, and gave them to Mr Home, who showed them to Drs Blair and Ferguson, by whom they were much admired. It turned out that one of these fragments, 'The Death of Oscar;' was applicable to another Oscar than the son of Ossian, but on what ground does Mr Laing pronounce it a forgery? Does he mean to say that Macpherson never heard these poems recited in Gaelic as he took them down? if so, what is his authority?—what object could Macpherson have in deceiving Mr Home? Mr Laing says, "That he could not resist the temptation to vindicate that neglected merit of which he was conscious by submitting *his own poetry*, which the public had hitherto overlooked, to a distinguished judge as a relic of antiquity." But as the translation was in prose and not in poetry, the whole of Mr Laing's visionary theory of fabrication falls to the ground. In the very next paragraph Mr Laing says, on the authority of a Mr Laurie, who pretends to have letters from Mr Macpherson, which are not produced, " that his Highland pride was alarmed at appearing only as a translator to the world." Where, then, was "the temptation," which, according to Mr Laing, "he could not resist"—the temptation to represent " his own poetry as a relic of antiquity"?

Dr Blair obtained from Macpherson a translation of all the fragments he had, being fifteen in number, and

published them in 1760, with a preface by himself, in
which he states, " They may depend on the following
fragments as genuine remains of ancient Scottish
poetry." On this Mr Laing remarks, " Without once
reflecting that the pretended translator was himself a
poet." Thereby implying that these translations were
forgeries of Macpherson's, and that the originals never
existed. On what grounds Mr Laing comes to this
conclusion he does not explain. He knew nothing of
the lower class of Highlanders ; he was ignorant of their
language, and had no means personally of ascertaining
whether these fragments were recited by them or not ;
and if he could have learned from others that such was
the case, he was incapable of appreciating their beauty
or the accuracy of the translation. But, unfortunately
for Mr Laing's theory, the Highland Society's Committee have recovered ample evidence of some of these
fragments being recited in Gaelic both before and after
the translation of them was published, and previous to
the publication of them in Gaelic. We have before us
the small octavo volume printed in 1760 which contains those 15 pieces, all of them very short. We have
compared them with the English Ossian, and find
most of them there reproduced ; Nos. 1, 2, 4, and 5 form
parts of Carric-thura ; 10, 11, and 12 form part of the
Songs of Selma, and 13, 14, and 15 part of Fingal ;
Nos. 3, 6, 7, 8, and 9 are not there reproduced, being
supposed to be more modern, yet one of them, No. 6,
Dargo, is shown by the already-quoted evidence to have
been recited in the Highlands, though the Gaelic original of it has never been given to the public. So much

for this allegation of forgery. Mr Laing, however, on the baseless assumption of the forgery, proceeds :

"From the first forgery of the death of Oscar, Macpherson was conducted, step by step, to other fabrications, by their (Home and Blair) importunity and zeal." Having thus asserted, without any grounds whatever, that the death of Oscar, and, in fact, all the fragments, were forgeries, and having assumed these false premises, Mr Laing goes on to reason out his own conclusions—with what candour we shall presently see.

But let us look for a moment at what Dr Carlyle, who was from the first conversant with all Macpherson's doings, says in regard to the fragments :

"As before this accidental meeting with Mr Home Mr Macpherson had no idea of collecting and translating the works of Ossian, the fact remained on my mind as a strong groundwork for the evidence of the authenticity of Ossian, when both the internal and external evidence was so ably scrutinised by Dr Blair. Upon this ground I remain fully convinced that Macpherson did not and could not, with all his ability, which was great, fabricate the poems ; though I am ready to admit that, after collecting all the scattered fragments he tied them together in form of heroic poems, as Homer is said to have done when he collected the songs of the Bards of Greece.

"Macpherson, however, had laid himself too much open to the critics by attempting in his 'Dissertations on Fingal' to unite two things that must remain separate—viz., poetical fiction and historical truth—which, I observe, has opened a late violent attack on him by a

writer of history, which, I have little doubt, will prove
as ineffectual to overthrow the authenticity of Ossian
as any of the former attacks." We need scarcely say
the writer of history here referred to is Mr Laing.

But Mr Laing goes further, and calls in Macpherson
himself to his aid, who, he says, "did not conceal the
fact from those with whom he was particularly intimate that the poems were entirely his own composition."
This he states on the authority of a note said to have
been addressed by the Bishop of Dromore to Dr Robert
Anderson of Edinburgh. We have not this note *in ex-
tenso*, nor have we Dr Anderson's letter to Mr Laing,
but we quote what is given by Mr Laing of the Bishop's
note : "The Bishop of Dromore has allowed Dr Anderson to declare that he repeatedly received the most
positive assurances from *Sir John Elliot*, the confiden-
tial friend of Macpherson, that all the poems published
by him as translations of Ossian were entirely of his
own composition." We should have liked that this
note or letter, which is said to have been dated April
16th 1805, had been given by Mr Laing at full length
—as he particularly requested the Highland Society's
Committee to do in their report of the letters which
they received—for there is some ambiguity in the
phraseology. It does not appear (though the inference
is suggested) that Sir John Elliot had ever been told by
Macpherson that he was the author, though Sir John
appears to have been of opinion that he was the author,
and to have said so to the Bishop ; nor is there, apart
from this letter, any evidence of Sir John's intimacy
with Macpherson, though we are aware of the intimacy

of both Bishop Percy and Dr Anderson with Dr Johnson, and of the obligations they were under to him, the
one in the collection of the 'Reliques,' and the other
in his edition of the Poets. It will also be observed
that in this note the Bishop gives no opinion of his own
as to the authorship; but in his preface to his 'Reliques'
he states the significant fact not noticed by Mr Laing,
that he had caused persons who had never any access
to see the translation to give the meaning of those
pieces which they repeated, and found the interpretation
which he got extempore correspond with the English
translation. But, after all, the opinion of Sir John
Elliot is not to be put for a moment in competition with
the direct evidence of Strathmashie or Captain Morison,
of Dr Blair or Dr Carlyle. On this point Dr Carlyle
says :*

"During my intimacy with Macpherson for two
winters in London in 1769 and 1770, when I saw him
daily, and lived in intimacy with him for four months
in each of those seasons, I never was able to discover
in his unguarded moments that he was any other than
the collector and translator of the works of Ossian, or
assumed any other merit than might be derived from
thence; but I have heard him express the greatest con-
tempt and disdain for those who thought him the fabri-
cator of them."

That Macpherson either admitted or asserted that his
Ossian was entirely composed by himself, and not made
up of translations of ancient Gaelic poetry, is not only
unsupported by any reliable evidence, but is simply

* See H. S. R., p. 66.

incredible, 1st, Because he could have been so easily contradicted and exposed by those who assisted him in the collecting and translating; and, 2dly, Because, if he had harboured any desire to be so regarded, he would not have preserved any of the Gaelic versions from which he had translated, and would not have instructed his executor to publish them, nor have left £1000 to defray the expense of the publication. Equally strained and futile is Mr Laing's attempt to draw from Macpherson's desire to be buried in Westminster Abbey the extraordinary inference that he thereby virtually admitted himself to have been guilty of the imposture imputed to him. Nor is the reference to certain passages in one of Macpherson's prefaces for the same purpose more successful. The passages apparently most relied on are the following, which occur in the last preface to his works in 1773:

" Without increasing his genius, the author may have improved his language in the eleven years that the following poems have been in the hands of the public. Errors in diction might have been committed at twenty-four which the experience of a riper age may remove; and some exuberances in imagery may be restrained with advantage by a degree of judgment acquired in the progress of time. Impressed with this opinion, he ran over the whole with attention and accuracy; and he hopes he has brought the work to a state of correctness which will preclude all future improvements." This clearly applies to Macpherson's own work, the English translation, which was thought rather flowery, and not to the Gaelic original.

In the other paragraph which follows he says: "When a composition cannot bear the test of a literal version, it is a counterfeit which ought not to pass current. The operation must, however, be performed with skilful hands: a translator who cannot equal his original is incapable of expressing its beauties." This is perfectly true, and is only meant to illustrate the proposition, that unless a translation is done by such skilful hands as to come up to the original, it is incapable of expressing its beauties; and when coupled with another paragraph in the same preface, shows distinctly that Macpherson never meant to give out to the public that he was the author of the Gaelic Ossian. Alluding to his persecution by the *English* critics, he says: "When rivers define the limits of abilities as well as the boundaries of countries, a writer may measure his success by the latitude under which he was born. It was to avoid a part of this inconvenience that the author *is said, by some who speak without any authority,* to have ascribed his own productions to another name. If this was the case, *he was but young in the art of deception.* When he placed *the poet* in antiquity, *the translator* should have been born on this side of the Tweed."

Mr Laing deals with Dr Blair's investigation thus: "In consequence of Mr David Hume's letters, Blair wrote to the Highlands to procure attestations, and an *incoherent mass of evidence* was added to the Dissertation in an appendix, which Macpherson afterwards suppressed."

Mr Laing has no objection to the loosest hearsay evidence when it suits his purpose; but when

distinct and direct evidence of the most undoubted
character is obtained which does not suit his views,
he passes it over as "an incoherent mass." He
admits, however, that there "are preserved in the
Highlands, by tradition or writing, about twenty or
thirty Irish ballads relative to the Fions, and ascribed
to Ossian," but says that they "are nothing superior
in point of poetical merit." There is no ground for
characterising these poems as Irish; some of them are
common to both Ireland and the Highlands, but some
are not, and they are generally less corrupted in Scotland than in Ireland, where they are interlarded with
romance, and some of the finest passages omitted. In
fact, these poems have been recited orally in Scotland,
where the language is more pure, to a much later period
than in Ireland. But Mr Laing says they have no
poetical merit. It has already been shown, and is
generally acknowledged, that the finest passages in
Macpherson's translation have been recovered in the
original; and as every one acquainted with both languages is aware that in the original these passages
are much superior to the translation, it would follow,
according to Mr Laing, that the translation must
be of no merit. Why, then, was it in the first
year after its publication translated into all the languages of Europe; and why did Mr Laing undertake
the task of reprinting it, and writing voluminous notes
on it? But Mr Laing's inconsistencies are endless.

Mr Laing further says,—"Johnson was informed,
about thirty years ago, that Macpherson, having made
some Erse translation from his English Ossian, had

taught a boy to write them, with injunctions to declare
that he had learned them from his grandmother; but
the boy when he grew up told the story." Mr Laing
gives this story apparently on the authority of Johnson,
and we must infer that he believes it, or wishes it to be
believed, more especially as he adds that "somewhat
of the same evidence is now obtruded upon the public."
Laing refers to a letter by Johnson to Boswell, of date
25th February 1775, which was, be it observed, immediately after Macpherson had threatened to chastise Johnson. On turning to the letter referred to, we
see the nature of the "information" which Mr Laing
regards as evidence of this absurd story. Johnson
describes it thus : " Macpherson *is said* to have made
some translations himself, and having taught a boy to
write it, ordered him to say that he had learned it of
his grandmother. The boy when he grew up told the
story. This Mrs Williams heard at Mr Strahan's
table." But from whom she heard it, or who the boy
was, or where he lived, or to whom he told the story
when he grew up, are not disclosed ; nor is it obvious
what object Macpherson could hope to accomplish by
such a wretched attempt at fraud. But even tea-table
gossip, as repeated by some old lady, was apparently
soothing to Johnson in his then state of mind ; and, for
want of something better, has been seized on by Mr
Laing with his usual avidity, and represented by him
as a veritable fact.

Let us now see how Mr Laing endeavours to support
his statement that "somewhat of the same evidence is
now obtruded upon the public."

"Sixteen lines" (says Mr Laing) "of Fingal in Erse are produced by Mr Gallie, an old clergyman of eighty, to whom they were furnished by a friend well acquainted with Gaelic, from the manuscript which Macpherson had formerly translated at the old gentleman's fireside. On applying to the latter for the name of his friend, ' so well known for his uncommon acquaintance with Gaelic,' I was informed that it was Mr Lachlan Macpherson of Strathmashie. This gentleman, in his letter to Blair, had attested without hesitation in 1763 that he had accompanied Macpherson in his journey through the Highlands, and assisted in collecting the poems of Ossian; that he took down from oral tradition, and transcribed from old manuscripts, by far the greatest part of those pieces that were published; that he had since compared the translations with the copies of the originals still in his hands, and found them so amazingly literal as to preserve even the cadence of the Gaelic versification; that some of the hereditary bards had committed very early to writing some of the works of Ossian, and that one manuscript in particular, which he saw in Macpherson's possession, was written so far back as 1410. Instead of appearing in person to produce those copies of the originals which remained in his hands, and to attest to the world from what particular manuscripts, extant or lost, or from whose oral recitation he had transcribed them, this gentleman, the kinsman, friend, and amanuensis of Macpherson, and a brother poet, had furnished Mr Gallie with sixteen lines of the *Erse version of Fingal made at his fireside*, without suspecting that the latter would ever divulge the secret from whom the lines had been originally procured."

We are at a loss to perceive any fraud in Mr Gallie applying to Mr L. Macpherson of Strathmashie (who had a number of James Macpherson's manuscripts) for a copy of the translation made at his (Mr Gallie's) fireside by James Macpherson and himself, and also for an extract from the original Gaelic manuscript of the portion so translated; nor was there anything wrong in Strathmashie furnishing it, nor any reason for concealment, nor attempt at it; but if Mr Laing means, as he appears to say, that the *Gaelic lines were made* at Mr Gallie's fireside, he not merely perverts evidence, but asserts without authority what is in direct opposition to the facts as stated in Mr Gallie's letters quoted above. Mr Laing continues:

"In a liberal and, to men of letters, an interesting controversy, *which I have happily divested of its former acrimony*, it is painful to animadvert upon those disingenuous arts to which anonymous writers are so apt to resort. But when *the parole evidence amounts to nothing*, the question returns with additional force,— Where are the manuscripts which Macpherson certainly collected in the Highlands?" It is rather ludicrous that Mr Laing should thus take credit for having divested the controversy of acrimony when he not only casts doubts on the testimony of every one who has given evidence as to the authenticity of these poems, and ignores the whole parole proof, but indulges in insinuations against the veracity of such gentlemen as Strathmashie and Captain Morison, applies the word "impostor" to Macpherson, and sneers at Drs Blair and Ferguson.

In his dissertation, published in 1800, Mr Laing says,—" If a single poem of Ossian in manuscript, such as translated by Macpherson, of a decent length, and the MS. indisputably of an older date than the present century, be produced and lodged in a public library, I shall return among the first to our national creed." In answer to this challenge, we would refer to the Death of Oscar in " Temora," and the episode of Fainesolis in "Fingal," and the poem of " Carthon," contained in the Dean of Lismore's book, of date 1512, now in the Advocates' Library, and which, though varying somewhat from Macpherson's version, are in fact but different editions of the same poems.

Mr Laing, in speaking of the twenty or thirty ballads previously alluded to (which he is pleased to call Irish), says : " The date of these poems must be ascribed to the fourteenth or fifteenth century, not only from internal evidence, but because Irish poetry is not once mentioned in the twelfth century by Giraldus Cambrensis;" and in his dissertation he says, " Rhymes in Welsh poetry were unknown to Giraldus Cambrensis in the twelfth century."

Unfortunately for Mr Laing's accuracy there occurs a well-known passage in which Giraldus expressly affirms that the Welsh excelled in rhymes :

" In cantilenis rythmicis et dictamine, tam subtiles inveniuntur, ut miræ et exquisitæ inventionis, tam verborum quam sententiarum proferant exornationis unde et poetas (quos bardos vocant) ad hoc deputatos multos invenias." * That is: "They are found so polished in rhyming ditties and in expression that they produce beauties of words and sentiment of wonderful and exquisite invention ; whence you find poets amongst them (whom they call bards) appointed for the purpose."

The passage is important, not only as affording another proof of the inaccuracy and recklessness of Mr Laing's assertions, but also as showing that, from the nicety (subtilis) and perfection to which the Welsh had, in the days of Giraldus, carried the invention of rhyme, its use amongst them must necessarily have been of great antiquity.

Under the head of " Manners and Customs," Mr Laing in his dissertation urges some strange elements of detection, which it will not be difficult to refute.

He remarks that the aspen, or trembling poplar, the *Crithean* of the Celts, so often mentioned in these poems, is a foreign tree, and not a native of Scotland. Here it appears that the learned gentleman chose to occupy ground to which he was a stranger, being a native of Orkney, where neither trees grow nor Gaelic is spoken. It is a point sufficiently established amongst naturalists, that the *populus tremula*, or aspen, is indigenous to Scotland. It can be pointed out in the utmost profusion in the Highlands, growing on the margin of lakes and in the crevices of rocks in almost every glen.

With equal gratuitousness the yew-tree, the *Iubhar* of the Highlanders, is asserted to be " certainly not

* Giraldus Cambrensis Itinerarium Cambriæ. Edit. London, 4to, p. 197.

indigenous." But it is certain that the yew-tree has
always been, and still is, a native of Scotland. Light-
foot, in his 'Flora Scotica,' holds it to be such, and
cites the authority of Dr Stuart of Luss, one of the first
names in the science of plants of his native Highlands.
There are innumerable places in Scotland which still
have their denomination from this tree, according to the
ordinary use of giving names to places from the species
of trees with which they abound — thus, *Glen-iu'ir*,
" the glen of yews ;" *Dunure*, " the hill of yews," &c. ;
and Giraldus Cambrensis informs us that the yew-tree
grew in such abundance in Ireland that the scarcity of
bees in that country is in part to be ascribed to this
cause.

It would be endless to follow Mr Laing through the
vague similarities which he adduces between certain
passages of Ossian and the ancient and modern classics.
There is throughout a forced assimilation of images and
expressions, which either have nothing in common, or
of which the resemblances may be easily accounted for.
We give one or two specimens.

In the poem of ' Cath-Loda ' the following description
is given of Strina-dona :

" If on the heath she moved, her breast was whiter
than the down of Cana ; if on the sea-beat shore, than
the foam of the rolling ocean."

Did we not know Mr Laing to be serious, it would
seem that he intended a burlesque upon criticism when
maintaining that the

" Seu solvit crines, fusis decet esse capillis"

of Tibullus—literally, " If she loosens her hair it be-
comes her to have flowing locks"—is the original of
Ossian's " If on the heath she moved, her breast was
whiter than the down of Cana ;" or when he again
maintains that Tibullus's

> " Seu compsit, comptis est veneranda comis
> —Urit seu nivea, urit seu tyria"—

that is, " If she adorn her hair she is graceful with
adorned locks—she inflames whether she is in white or
in purple"—is the original of Ossian's " If on the sea-
beat shore, than the foam of the rolling ocean." In
these alleged imitations nothing common can be de-
cerned except the particle *seu* in the Latin, and *if* in
the English. Again, Ossian's " Her dark hair flowed
round it in streaming clouds" is, with Mr Laing, Tibullus's

> " Fusis decet esse capillis."

Surely the learned gentleman imagined that his
readers could not translate Tibullus, or that they would
be too indolent to compare the alleged resemblances.

Let us now view this controversy from the Gaelic
side of the question.

Macpherson's translation had been so eulogised, and
had created such a sensation, that the applause of the
public was quite exhausted, and when the Gaelic version appeared forty years afterwards, being of interest
to only a limited number, it was little noticed. It has,
however, a material bearing on this controversy.

It is well known that Macpherson, having left the Highlands at an early age, devoted his attention much to classical studies, and was no great Gaelic scholar. He could read and translate the language, and had a just appreciation of its beauties, but in conversation he made great blunders, and was quite unable to write it accurately, far less to compose Gaelic poetry. On this point we have ample authority.

Ewan Macpherson, who accompanied James Macpherson on part of his tour, mentions that in Uist they met with MacCodrum the poet, and that Macpherson asked him, " *A bheil dad agad air an Fhéinn?* " by which he meant to inquire whether or not he knew any of the poems of Ossian relative to the Fingalians. But the terms in which the question was asked strictly imported whether or not the Fingalians owed him anything; and MacCodrum, being a man of humour, took advantage of the blunder, and answered that really if they had owed him anything the bonds and obligations were lost, and he believed any attempt to recover them at that time of day would be unavailing. This sally of MacCodrum's wit seemed to have hurt Mr Macpherson, who cut short the conversation and proceeded towards Benbecula.

On the authority of Captain Morison, who assisted Macpherson in translating and transcribing from the original manuscripts, the late Rev. Mr Irvine of Little Dunkeld, in a letter to the Rev. Patrick Graham of Aberfoyle,* says : " Mr Morison assures me that Mr Macpherson understood the Gaelic language very imper-

* See Graham's Essay on the Authenticity of Ossian, p. 284.

fectly; that he (Mr Morison) wrote out the Gaelic for him, for the most part, on account of Mr Macpherson's inability to write or spell it properly; that Mr Morison assisted him much in translating; and that it was their general practice when any passages occurred which they did not well understand, either to pass it over entirely, or to gloss it over with any expressions that might appear to coalesce easily."

And, in answer to the inquiries of the Highland Society's Committee, Captain Morison says: * " That he was intimately acquainted with his abilities and know- ledge of the Gaelic language; he admits that he had much merit in collecting and arranging and translating, but that, so far from composing such poems as were translated, he assisted him often in understanding some words, and suggested some improvements."

It is therefore impossible that he could be the author of that highly-finished Gaelic verse which has been communicated to the public. But, further, his want of knowledge of Gaelic words appears even in his trans- lations, of which there is a striking instance in the poem of 'Carricthura.' It occurs in the description of Fingal's celebrated combat with the Spirit of Loda. The spirit having boasted that he dwelt undisturbed in his pleasant plains in the clouds, Fingal thus replies:

" Gabhsa còmhnuidh na do raoin,
    Thuirt righ nach b'fhaoin, 's a làmh air beairt,
    Neo cuimhnich MacChumhail air raon;
    'S lag do thannas; 's mòr mo neart."

* See H. S. R., App., p. 177.

This, with the addition of two words in italics, is literally :

" Take up thy abode in thy plains *of air*,
    Said the not vain king with his hand on his weapon,
    Else remember the son of Comhal on the plain,
    Feeble is thy shade ; great is my might."

This whole passage Macpherson translates in these words—" Dwell in thy pleasant fields, said the king ; let Comhal's son be forgot."

Here it is evident that Macpherson has totally misunderstood the term *neo* in the third line, and which here signifies, else or otherwise ; translating it as if it were the particle *neo*, which, compounded with an adjective, has in Gaelic the force of the English particle *un* in " unfaithful," and converts the term to which it is added into an opposite sense.   Thus the adjective *ciontach*, " guilty," with the particle *neo* prefixed to it (neo-chiontach), signifies " not guilty" or " innocent." In consequence of this egregious mistake, the translator has completely lost the sense of the original, and makes the undaunted Fingal solicit a compromise with the Spirit of Loda altogether unworthy of his character.   It is as if he had said, " Let me go, and I shall let thee go."   But to make this sense of the passage tolerable, Mr Macpherson finds himself under the necessity of omitting the greatest part of the line immediately preceding, and the whole of the line which follows.

The question then arises, Who composed the Gaelic Ossian ?   After a careful examination of these poems,

we feel satisfied that, though there are a few inaccurate
expressions in them, no one of modern times could
have produced them.

It is generally admitted that the language of the
Highlands of Scotland has not suffered much change
since the original settlement of the Celts in these re-
gions. Except in their encounters with the Romans,
and the temporary incursions of the Danes in a subsequent period, they had, for a long series of ages, no
intercourse by conquest or by commerce with any other
country but Ireland, whose language was the same
with their own.

This appears very distinctly in the songs of the
bards, who, from the days of " *Iain Lom*" (the bard of
Montrose) down to the present day, wrote in precisely
the same language as is now spoken in those districts
where the dialect is pure ; and this also may be said of
some compositions of an earlier date, such as ' *Miann
a Bhaird Aosda*,' or 'The Aged Bard's Wish,' which,
for beauty and simplicity of composition, is equal to
Wordsworth's best style. We give a few stanzas (not
continuous). The scene appears to be laid in the Braes
of Lochaber. The dialect is the same as is now spoken
there :

O càraibh mi ri taobh nan allt,
A shiubhlas mall le ceumaibh ciùin,
Fo sgàil a bharraich leag mo cheann,
'S bi thùs'a ghrian ro-chairdeil rium.

" Mu'n cuairt do bhruachaibh àrd mo ghlinn
Biodh lùbadh ghéug a's orra blàth ;

'S clann bheag nam preas a' tabhairt seinn
Do chreagaibh aosd 'le 'oran gràidh.

" O, ceum an t-sealgair ri mo chluais !
Le sranna ghàth a's chon feagh sléibh
'N sin dearsaidh an 'òig air mo ghruaidh,
'N uair dh-eireas toirm air sealg na fhéidh.

" Thig le càirdeas thar a chuain
Osag mhin a ghluais gu mall,
Tog mo cheò air sgiath do luathais,
'S imich grad gu Eilean Fhlaitheis,

" Far'm beil na laoich a dh-fhalbh o shean,
An cadal trom gun dol le ceòl,
Fosglaibh-sa thalla Oisein a's Dhaoil,
Thig an oidhche's cha bhi'm bàrd air bhrath."

Literal Translation.

"O place me near the brooks which slowly move
with gentle steps. Under the shade of the branches
lay my head, and be thou, O Sun, very friendly to me."

" Around the lofty brow of my glen let there be bending boughs in full bloom, and the children of the bushes
making the aged rocks re-echo their songs of love."

" O let me hear the hunter's step, with the sound of
his darts, and the noise of his dogs throughout the
hills; then youth shall beam on my cheek, when the
din of hunting the deer shall arise."

"Come with friendship over the sea, O soft blast that slowly movest ; bear my shade on the wing of thy swiftness, and travel quickly to the Isle of Heroes,"

" Where the brave that went of old are deep in slumber, without music. Open, ye halls of Ossian and Daol. The night shall come and the bard shall not be found."

From the allusion here to the Isle of Heroes, and other passages in this poem, which is of considerable length, it is plain that it must have been of an early date, and probably many centuries old ; but from the mention of cattle and goats, and the style of the composition, it must have been subsequent to the era of Ossianic poetry. In fact the Ossianic poetry stands alone, quite distinct and separate from all other Gaelic poetry. It is heroic in its character, and differs from all other poetical compositions which can be traced for some centuries back in style, sentiment, and language. The grandeur of its similes, the vividness of its descriptions, and the simplicity and polish of its diction, and, we must add, the number of obsolete words used, stamp the poetry of Ossian as of an earlier date than any other that has reached us. We do not therefore wonder that Captain Morison, who assisted in transcribing and translating these poems, when asked by the Committee of the Highland Society whether Macpherson could have composed them, should have answered, " That he could as well compose the Prophecies of Isaiah, or create the island of Skye."

No doubt Macpherson had the assistance of Captain
Morison and Strathmashie in translating, transcribing,
and arranging. But Captain Morison was no poet; Macpherson never wrote a line of Gaelic poetry in his life ;
and Strathmashie, judging from the few songs he has
written, was a poet of a very secondary class. We
therefore concur with Dr Blair that, though these poems
were not found in the connected form in which they
are now presented to the public, but were collected from
different manuscripts, and from oral recitation, as described by Macpherson himself, yet they exhibit, " as
they stand, a genuine, authentic view of ancient Gaelic
poetry."

To the criticisms on the particular form of verse we
do not attach much importance. In Gaelic poetry
the rhyme, if such it may be called, is peculiar, and is
rather a harmony of sound or cadence which pleases
the ear. The verse in which Ossian is composed
consists of eight feet, and is well suited for heroic
poetry ; but Gaelic is a language so well adapted, from
its great flexibility, for composition in verse, that we find
in Gaelic songs all sorts of measures adopted, and even
some in imitation of pipe-music. These are composed
from the ear; and though, perhaps, rules might be de-
duced for the formation of any kind of verse, yet we
cannot go into the complicated theories of Mr Davies
and others on the subject, which were never understood
by some of the best Gaelic poets of even modern times,
many of whom could neither read, write, nor speak
English.

The superiority of the Gaelic version of the Ossianic

poems over the English translation is one of the strongest arguments in favour of their authenticity, but it is
one which, though it may be inferred by all, can only
be fully felt by those acquainted with both languages,
and therefore the supporters of the authenticity of
Ossian have had reason to complain that they had
suffered more from the ignorance than from the knowledge of their opponents.

In order to appreciate with tolerable accuracy the
mode in which Macpherson proceeded in the arrange-
ment of his materials, we may mention, what is well
known to many, that before the Highland reciter delivers
his poem he generally prefaces it with a short summary,
in a kind of measured prose, of the principal events
contained in the verses which he is about to recite.
This outline of the poem is called the *Sgeulachd* or tale.
By the help of this outline Macpherson seems to have
been enabled at least to connect in regular order the
several detached pieces which he found in tradition
according to the series of events to which they related.
When a poem occurred which could not by this
method be made to coalesce with his larger work, he
seems to have proceeded by two ways—he either gives
the poem in its detached state as he found it, and as
the lesser poems now appear in his publication, or he
introduces it as an episode, as he has done in the instance
of the 'Maid of Craca,' and in that of the expedition of
Carthon in the close of the Seventh Book of 'Temora.'
Of such episodes, indeed, skilfully introduced, and in
general allied to the subject of the work, a great portion
of 'Fingal' and 'Temora' consists.

As to the inference attempted to be rested on Macpherson's taciturnity, we may here quote from a passage in Dr Blair's letter to Mr Mackenzie, 20th December 1797:* "For my own part, from my perfect knowledge of all the circumstances of their discovery and translation, it was impossible for me to entertain any doubts on the subject of their authenticity. Of all men I ever knew Mr Macpherson was the most unlikely and unfit to contrive and carry on such an imposture as some people in England ascribed to him. He had none of the versatility, the art, and dissimulation which such a character and such an undertaking would have required. He was proud, high-spirited, and disdainful; irritable to a degree when his honour and veracity were impeached; not very apt on any occasion to listen to advice; and when unjust censures were thrown out against him, obstinate in his purpose of disregarding and contemning them, without the least concern of giving any satisfaction to those who opposed or cavilled at him."

Were Macpherson even more inclined to be communicative than he was, we are at a loss to conjecture how he could have satisfied further inquiry as to the originality of these poems; for it must be kept in mind that they were not found in one continuous whole, but were in detached pieces, as collected by himself or others in the Highlands, or scattered through the pages of old manuscripts, written in a language and in a character intelligible to but few. He had fully stated to the public in his prefaces how they had been ob-

* H. S. R. App., p. 56.

tained, and in this he had been corroborated by Dr
Blair, who took an active part in their collection, and
who published a dissertation on the subject, and while
he declined to appeal to the testimony of those who
aided him in their collection, he allowed Blair to do so.
Yielding, however, to advice, he placed the manuscripts
in Becket's shop for public inspection, and advertised
that he had done so. Nor is it to be forgotten that
those to whom he had submitted them privately were
the persons best qualified to judge of their authenticity.

We have thus shown :

1. That Macpherson collected manuscripts containing
Ossianic poetry, which he was assisted in transcribing
and translating by friends who testify to the fact.

2. That he also collected a number of Ossianic poems
from recitation, which were taken down by gentlemen
who accompanied him in his search and acted as his
amanuenses.

3. That he received several Ossianic poems from
friends.

4. That he was by no means a good Gaelic scholar,
and required the assistance of friends to translate for
him, and that he often mistook the meaning of the
original.

5. That subsequent to the publication of the English Ossian, but many years before that of the Gaelic
poems, a large portion of the finest parts of the poems
translated by him were recovered in the original,
partly from private collections, but principally from the
recitation of persons who could neither read nor write.

6. That previous to the publication of these Gaelic poems, a large number of other Ossianic poems not published by Macpherson were collected and given to the public in the original, many of which are as fine as any of those published by him.

7. That the original poetry translated by Macpherson contains a number of obsolete words not to be found in any modern poetry, and that as a composition it is much superior to his translation.

8. That Macpherson openly avowed that his larger poems were compiled from detached poems arranged by him, which had been collected from old manuscripts, from recitation, and from ancient poems sent him by friends, and that he himself gave them the name of Epic.

At what date Ossian lived we do not pretend to determine; but this, at least, is sufficiently clear, that the Gaelic Ossian was not the production of Macpherson or any author of modern times, but must be referred to a period of remote antiquity. It further appears, from the internal evidence of these poems, that they refer to a period prior to the diffusion of Christianity and the era of clanship in the Highlands.

.